WHAT "MUFFIN" LOVERS ACROSS THE COU

The Thomas J. O'Connor Animal Control and Adoption Center and its foundation applauds the values expressed in Mrs. Eckroat's book, which showcases the importance of adopting a pet and supporting your local animal shelter.

—Thomas J. O'Connor Animal Control and Adoption Center, Springfield, MA

Went Out to Get a Donut is a fun book to read to your child while at the same time introducing the importance of adopting and rescuing animals. Mrs. Eckroat helps start the conversations with this book.

—Sherwin Daryani, Executive Director, Operation Kindness, Carrolton, TX

Went Out to Get a Donut is a charming, whimsical way to engage the littlest readers into the importance of animal rescue. I recommend this book to parents and teachers everywhere who want to add some humane education to their reading repertoire.

—Michelle Sathe, Author, *Pit Stops: Crossing the Country with Loren the Rescue Bully*
Board Member of The Brittany Foundation and Bow-Wows and Meows, Inc.

… *Came Home With a Muffin* will win the hearts of children of all ages. The story behind the story is equally engaging and charming. It will become a favorite for dog lovers everywhere.

—Carolyn Hedgecock, Haltom City, TX, Author, *Locker Letters*

Published by Tate Publishing & Enterprises, LLC
127 E. Trade Center Terrace | Mustang, Oklahoma 73064 USA
1.888.361.9473 | www.tatepublishing.com

Tate Publishing is committed to excellence in the publishing industry. The company reflects the philosophy established by the founders, based on Psalm 68:11,
"The Lord gave the word and great was the company of those who published it."

Book design copyright © 2011 by Tate Publishing, LLC. All rights reserved.
Cover and interior design by Chris Webb
Illustrations by Greg White

Published in the United States of America

ISBN: 978-1-61346-841-8
1. Juvenile Fiction / Animals / Dogs
2. Juvenile Fiction / Animals / General
11.11.1

Went Out To Get **A DONUT—**
Came Home With **A MUFFIN**

WRITTEN BY
LAURA W. ECKROAT

ILLUSTRATED BY
GREG WHITE

tate publishing
CHILDREN'S DIVISION

FOREWORD

Laura Eckroat's children's book presents a valuable teachable opportunity about the plight of companion animals in this country. Muffin, the lead character, represents the millions of dogs, cats, rabbits, and other small animals that are abandoned or left homeless every year.

While the numbers of homeless animals are staggering, the news is good—life-giving solutions to animal overpopulation and homelessness are making a difference in communities across the country. Advocates are turning the tide by providing affordable spay or neuter surgery, behavioral and veterinary intervention, humane education lessons for children, and the information and tools people need to keep animals in their homes. Yet none of these is as meaningful a solution to an individual animal at risk as a life-saving adoption.

Laura uses the vehicle of children's literature to tell a simple story of rescue. In doing so, she gives parents and caregivers the opportunity to teach children about caring for animals—a lesson that stands firmly in opposition to the neglect of animals in this country. I hope the story of Muffin will continue to provide those teachable moments and advocate for the selfless act of adopting a sheltered animal.

Opening our hearts and homes to an animal in need is the first step in creating a truly humane society. Our thanks to Laura Eckroat for her words and message. Her compassion for animals will bring to many homes the love with which she writes.

—Leslie Harris, Executive Director
Dakin Pioneer Valley Humane Society
Springfield and Leverett, Massachusetts

DEDICATION

To Steven, Ashley, and Muffin—who have listened to this story a million times and have the tune stuck in their heads. And, to everyone who has supported my writing—I truly appreciate you! To Greg White, my illustrator, who gets into my head and does what my hands could never do! And Mabel, the sweetest Beagle, who is now at peace with her buddy Scooby; they are both Muffin's guardian angels.

Oh... I went to the store to buy a donut,
A strawberry, jelly-filled, tasty donut.
I went to the store to buy a donut—
but I came home with a Muffin.

Oh...I went to the store to buy a donut,
A sugary, twisty, tasty donut.
I went to the store to buy a donut—
but I came home with a Muffin.

Oh…I went to the store to buy a donut,
A chocolate, frosted, tasty donut.
I went to the store to buy a donut—
but I came home with a Muffin.

Oh…I went to the store to buy a donut,
A coconut-ty, sweet, tasty donut.
I went to the store to buy a donut—
but I came home with a Muffin.

Oh... I went to the store to buy a donut,
A chock-full of blueberry, tasty donut.
I went to the store to buy a donut—
but I came home with a Muffin.

Oh... I went to the store to buy a donut,
An old-fashioned, cakey, tasty donut.
I went to the store to buy a donut—
but I came home with a Muffin.

Oh... I went to the store to buy a donut,
A cinnamon, sugary, tasty donut.
I went to the store to buy a donut—
but I came home with a Muffin.

Oh... I went to the store to buy a donut,
A Boston, creamy, oozy, tasty donut.
I went to the store to buy a donut—
but I came home with a Muffin.

Oh... I went to the store to buy a donut,
An apple cider, tasty donut.
I went to the store to buy a donut—
but I came home with a Muffin.

Oh... I went to the store to buy a donut,
A powered, sugary, tasty donut.
I went to the store to buy a donut—
but I came home with a Muffin.

Oh... I went to the store to buy a donut,
A double-chocolaty, tasty donut.
I went to the store to buy a donut—
but I came home with a Muffin.

Oh... I went to the store to buy a donut,
A vanilla, sprinkled, tasty donut.
I went to the store to buy a donut—
but I came home with a Muffin.

Oh... I went to the store to buy some donuts,
But I turned the corner and spotted some schmutts,
Some wonderfully, floppy-eared, joyful pups.
I went to the store to buy some donuts, but I came home
with Muffin.

She's a rescue dog, and you know what?
She's full of love, my Muffin mutt.
Her nose is cold, and her paws are big,
And she uses them to dig.

But I love her so, and she is mine.
She loves to chase leaves, and that's just fine.
She doesn't beg at the table, yeah right!
And her best friend's a beagle named Mabel...

Oh...I went to the store to buy some donuts,
And I'm glad I came home with Muffin!

MUFFIN'S STORY

In March of 2010, we had to put down our wonderful rescue dog named Scooby; our hearts were sad, and we did not want to get another dog "just to replace her." We also had Mabel, our couch-potato beagle who missed having her best friend around. We were in the process of moving from Massachusetts to Texas—not a good time to get a new puppy.

Once the move was complete and we were in our new home, Mabel still seemed lost and still was grieving the loss of Scooby, as were we. Compounded by the move, Mabel was one sad beagle.

On a scorching Sunday in August 2010, we searched the Internet looking at rescue dogs. They were all adorable, but one captured our attention and immediately captured my heart. We drove twenty-plus miles to meet this tiny little pup we saw on the Internet.

Muffin was brought to the rescue house by a foster mom. We met Muffin's brother and several other males. Muffin was the only female amongst many males. She was submissive, scared, and quiet, but she also appeared to be very smart. When Steven, my husband, set her down for a minute, she walked over to the gate and looked up at us as if to say "Hey … let's go. You're my new family!"

We came to find out that we would be the fourth home Muffin would be going to, and she was only twelve weeks old. She was taken from her mom at five weeks old and quickly learned how to survive on her own.

Muffin barely weighed eight pounds when we brought her home; she was skin, bones, and a little bit of fur—she had lost her fur from not being fed properly. She was malnourished, had fleas, was dehydrated and, we came to find out a few weeks later, had mange.

For the first few days at our house, Muffin didn't run, play, chew, cry like all new puppies do. She slept—a *lot!* And she drank lots of water, and when she was resting, she would lay by the water bowl—a very telling action by such a young pup.

We have nursed Muffin back to health, though she is still taking medicine for mange, it is clearing up nicely. She is now six months old and weighs sixty-one pounds—a far cry from the skin–and–bones pup we got at twelve weeks, and she is now full of energy. She is going to training class and enjoys it very much. She picks out toys at the pet store and carries them to the counter—very cute. But one of her most favorite things to do is to take walks. She loves romping after butterflies and grasshoppers and chasing leaves.

Muffin is a rescue dog…and we're glad we rescued her!

e|LIVE

---

listen|imagine|view|experience

AUDIO BOOK DOWNLOAD INCLUDED WITH THIS BOOK!

In your hands you hold a complete digital entertainment package. In addition to the paper version, you receive a free download of the audio version of this book. Simply use the code listed below when visiting our website. Once downloaded to your computer, you can listen to the book through your computer's speakers, burn it to an audio CD or save the file to your portable music device (such as Apple's popular iPod) and listen on the go!

How to get your free audio book digital download:

1. Visit www.tatepublishing.com and click on the e|LIVE logo on the home page.
2. Enter the following coupon code:
   c483-3a19-1d84-5c8d-ec9c-c496-8b30-2023
3. Download the audio book from your e|LIVE digital locker and begin enjoying your new digital entertainment package today!